Letters
from
Damascus

Letters from Damascus

A Pauline Short Story

Greg M. Dodd

HARVEST
CHRONICLES

ISBN-10: 0991533259
ISBN-13: 9780991533251 Paperback
Rolos Tuesday Publishing, Columbia, SC
Printed in the United States of America

"If I have a faith that can move mountains, but do not have love, I am nothing."

— The Apostle Paul, 1 Corinthians 13:2

PREFACE

Buried in the context of the Apostle Paul's New Testament letters – beneath the doctrine, instruction, encouragement and theology – is the story of a life. Paul's life. We know that from and through that life, God spoke to us. Not through abstract dictation, but through the filter of Paul's own experiences. His joy and pain, triumph and failure, hardship and heartbreak – all framed by the people closest to him – made Paul the man he was. But who was he?

Most of what we know about Paul came from his own hand. From Tarsus, in modern day Turkey, he was born the son of a Pharisee. First known as Saul, he was schooled by the renowned rabbi Gamaliel in Jerusalem. He was a tent maker. And like his father, he became a Pharisee. But there is so much more we do not know about Paul. What was the infamous "thorn in the flesh" mentioned in 2 Corinthians 12? Had he been married at some point, as some speculate? If so, what happened? And how could that have impacted his ministry? And what became of letters written to Paul? Surely, there were many. And who wrote them? What more would they reveal about the man God used to spread the Gospel to the world? Two thousand years later, we're left to wonder, discuss, debate, and suppose.

Letters from Damascus explores, in fictional terms, one plausible backstory for Paul's ministry, told in a way already familiar to us – through letters.

Greg M. Dodd
Columbia, SC 2017

CONTENTS

ONE

Saul, a humbled servant of the Almighty God, with exceeding love and devotion to Shiri, my beloved wife: May the grace and mercy of God the Father fall upon you and all who dwell in our household in Jerusalem.

It is with a heavy, yet renewed heart that I write you, my love, for I have been permitted to see the glory of God, for whom I have eagerly served with all my being, only to be found his opponent. I know now that whatever standing I had or thought I possessed before him was of my own making or that of foolish men. For I have met the one whom I have persecuted, Jesus of Nazareth. The one in whom these followers of the Way place their faith. The one we watched die on a Roman cross at our bidding. The one for whom so many lie in prison or beneath the earth as a result of my efforts.

This Jesus appeared to me on the road to Damascus; his glory shown around me and shook me from my feet. My dearest Shiri – he lives! And the full measure of his light exposed this truth: I have been fighting the good fight for the enemy's benefit.

Indeed, the very commission under which I journeyed to Damascus, that which brought much praise and honor from my fellow Pharisees and members of the Sanhedrin, proved nothing more than the work of Satan, himself. Yet God, in his infinite and mysterious mercy, chose to offer me grace, though I have toiled vigorously – with all pride, zeal and confidence – against his will. The stories of Jesus' resurrection, repeated by those we have openly mocked, cursed, and persecuted, are true and to which I now proclaim myself a witness. Therefore, I testify to this: Jesus is the Christ, the Messiah, the Son of the living God. And to him I pledge my allegiance and my life to whatever end it may bring.

That which I have done over these last five years I cannot undo; though I would now trade my life for those I saw put to death. I am not ill, my love, I swear it. Though, the light of his heavenly glory left me blind for three days. And in that darkness, the faces of those who suffered at my hand haunted me. No greater anguish consumed me than the memory of Stephen, of whose death I boasted prior to leaving you. His voice cried out, as I watched him die, praying to Jesus and asking God to forgive our transgression against him. Shiri, I killed Stephen for the faith I now possess! That God's grace and mercy should extend to me now is beyond my understanding, yet it is so. He has rescued me from the path of destruction. And I stand forever in his debt.

Were it possible to tell you these amazing things in person, my beloved, I would do so. But for now I remain hidden in Damascus, unsure of my fate. Those of my former alliance now actively seek my ruin. And my presence among the followers of the Way has caused much consternation, as many remain fearfully aware of my previous ambitions against them. Yet, I am grateful for the care, prayers, and watchful eye of one of their elders, who has taken me in and counted me among their own.

I long to come to you and share the good news of Jesus, that you may also receive the redeeming truth of which I speak. Please give your father my greetings, as well as Ilan, Dalia and my dear friend Simeon. And extend hospitality to Barnabas. He has journeyed to you from Damascus on my behalf.

May the grace of the Lord be with you. And may my love for you remain a treasure in your heart.

Saul

TWO

*Shiri, daughter of Gilead, to my husband, Saul:
Greetings.*

*Word of your stay in Damascus reached me
long before your letter. Indeed, rumors of your
betrayal to our people have filled my ears for
weeks, though I have faithfully defended my
husband's name to which I am bound. And yet,
words from your own hand make me a fool.
What strange work is this that you should
mourn sinners who died under your righteous
service to our Lord? I can only hope that you
have indeed fallen ill and are speaking from a
fevered mind.*

*We both know God chose you to put an end
to the Way by seeking out these blaspheming
followers of Jesus. When I petitioned my father to
speak on your behalf before the high priest
Ananias, that your request for letters to the
synagogues in Damascus might be granted, I
did so believing there was none more honorable
in all of Jerusalem than my husband. Your rival
among the Pharisees, Jaron, may speak with
great piety and excite people to oppose these
heretics, but even his grandest boasts cannot*

equal all you have done in service to our people. His words are loud, but his deeds are empty. Jerusalem's prisons overflow with followers of the Way by your works, not his. Yet, you are in hiding while he roams freely in the marketplace shouting lies against you. He claims that you preach Jesus in the synagogues of Damascus! But I am not convinced. Jealousy speaks whenever Jaron mentions your name; I am sure of it. For I have known you, Saul of Tarsus, since you came to Jerusalem as a boy and have loved no other. And until I see into your brown eyes and feel the warm breath of truth from your lips, I will not believe the words Jaron speaks against you. Nor will I believe the lies in your letter, for the man I love could not have written them.

My faith is in you, my love, and all that we have planned is still before us. A path of great prominence lies open before you. Do not destroy what God has prepared! My father has spoken with Gamaliel. We have his promise to help restore your name upon your return. However, his son, Simeon, your friend, has sworn an oath against you in defiance of his father. I would not count on his support. But I believe truth will defeat your enemies.

I am entrusting this letter to the one you sent, Barnabas, for he would not tell me where you are now. He claims openly to be a follower of

Jesus, but I told no one in the hope my letter would reach you safely. I must warn you, my love, of a growing number here in Jerusalem, led by Jaron, who speak of your death in wishful terms. If you do journey home to me, please do so in secret.

I pray for your safe return and sound mind.

Shiri

THREE

Saul, to my wife Shiri in Jerusalem: Grace and peace to you from God the Father and the risen Lord Jesus Christ.

I thank God for your loyalty and confidence in me. In my absence, you rightly defend that which you believe to be true: That your husband is a servant of the living God, defender of the faith and leader among men. I know you count these things among your treasured possessions and guard them in your heart. I expected nothing less from you. Indeed, your passion gave birth to my ambition; and from ambition came learning; from learning, knowledge; from knowledge, zeal; and from zeal, power. But the power I wielded in the name of God came from misguided, ignorant men who blindly oppose the truth. Truth lives in the name of Jesus, whom I now humbly and willingly serve. And the power entrusted to me to do God's will comes through him, not through men.

Please extend my respect and gratitude to your father and Gamaliel the Elder, though I release them from any defense of my name. While it grieves me to learn of Simeon's oath, I have no interest in or need for the approval of men. Let them say what they will; a higher calling now moves me.

The plans you mentioned, which I pursued so forcefully at the expense of many, I have cast aside. I leave them for fools like Jaron, who only seek attention and profit above others. My one ambition is this: To proclaim that Jesus Christ is Lord. Though Jaron may speak from jealousy – with that I agree – what he shouts in the marketplace is true: I preach the name of Jesus in the synagogues of Damascus. Since receiving God's grace, I can do nothing else. I preach so that eyes may be opened to the truth, so that God's people will turn from darkness to light and receive a place among those who are sanctified by faith in Christ Jesus.

The gospel I preach here I wish to bring home to you at God's appointed time. Until then, I urge you to remember our fathers' wisdom in choosing us, one for the other. The value of my father's dowry cannot compare with the love I have for you. Such is not always the case in marriage. (Your sister, Hannah, knows this too well.) Beware of vultures who seek to cast doubt in your mind about us. I remain faithful to the vow I made you. And if you indeed prayed as a child, as you have often claimed, that God would provide a husband of noble character, deep faith, and pure love, then your prayers have been answered. For I have been stripped of my pride, leaving only what noble righteousness God gives through his grace. My faith now draws from a deep, eternal spring, rising up from the name of Jesus. And my love for you flows from the pure heart of God. Therefore, be encouraged, my love, and be strong in the bond we share.

I plan to leave Damascus soon if I can find a way out of the city wall, as it is becoming too dangerous for me here. I long to return to Jerusalem, to hold your hand in mine and share this gift I have so undeservedly received. Be kind to Silas; he traveled at great risk to bring my words to you.

The grace of our Lord Jesus Christ be with you.

Saul

FOUR

Shiri, of the house of Gilead, to my husband Saul: I send you greetings, though I know not where this letter will find you. But I pray for your wellbeing and for God's mercy to fall upon you.

When our fathers brought us together, as you mentioned in your previous letter, I counted their wisdom as blessings designed by God. That I would wed such a man as you filled my heart with expectant hope and promise. And after my father arranged for your instruction under Gamaliel the Elder, you did not disappoint. I watched with pride as you grew in knowledge and fervor for scripture and the history of our people. Indeed, word spread throughout Jerusalem of my young husband's learning beyond his years. Your success even exceeded the petitions of my prayers. All this you have forsaken. And for what? A dead blasphemer from Nazareth and his sect of unschooled fishermen? You are more than that, my love! Omri once called you "a Hebrew of Hebrews"! Yet you throw away your gains as if they were dung.

What happened to you on the road to Damascus, I cannot explain. But what caused you to turn against your people and, in so doing, turn against me, I cannot accept. You have brought shame to my father's house and bitter disappointment to the one who loved you. When I first heard of your profession of faith in Jesus, I did not believe it, even when penned from your own hand. But the case against you is now undeniable. You affirmed as much in your last letter. Therefore, I ask, with the blessings of my father and the high priest Ananias, to be released from my vow of matrimony to you. As long as I bear your name, I cannot lift my eyes to another nor even bare my face in Jerusalem. I would rather endure the shame of divorce than the shame of remaining your wife. I submit, as I must, to your desires in this matter. But know this: In your absence and subject to your duplicity, I have been comforted by another. Jaron has remained faithful to his people and a respected leader among the Pharisees. He proudly carries the burden you so publically abandoned. And in my time of humiliation, he offered his hand in friendship for which I am grateful. I write these things so that you may know I no longer wait for your return.

Your messenger, Silas, while much younger than your friend Barnabas, is cut from the same cloth. He boasts of Jesus and of your conversion to the Way even over my displeasure in hearing it. Were I not in need of his feet to carry my letter to you, I would hand him over to Jaron to be dealt with properly.

I await your answer to my request. May God lead you justly in this matter.

Shiri

FIVE

Saul, servant of the living Lord Jesus Christ, to my wife in Jerusalem.

My dear Shiri, do you not realize that the God of your father, of Moses, of David, and the twelve tribes of Israel, is the same God I now serve through his Son, Jesus? The same God you accuse me of dishonoring? There is only one God. For it is written:

"And there is no other God besides Me,

A righteous God and a Savior;

There is none except Me.

Turn to Me and be saved,

all the ends of the earth;

For I am God, and there is no other."

This is the same God we have worshipped since we were weaned from our mothers' milk. It is the same God who sent prophet after prophet to the Hebrew people, but we would not listen. I myself knew the scriptures; I repeated the words of the prophets in the temple, yet even I did not heed their message. For I was blinded by my appetite for religion and the pursuits of men. But God, since creation, has promised a redeemer, a savior, a messiah for the people of Israel and all the world. Shiri, it has happened! God's promise is fulfilled in Christ Jesus. It is he of whom the profit Isaiah spoke. He walked among us but we rejected him.

> "He was pierced for our transgressions,
> he was crushed for our iniquities;
> the punishment that brought us peace was
> on him, and by his wounds we are healed."

That Jesus should suffer and die on a cross for my transgressions, yet be raised in glory to offer grace to one such as me, is beyond comprehension. Yet it is proof of God's love for even the lowest of sinners, of which I am the lowest. But I have seen God's redeemer with my own eyes. He has taken the sword from my hand and has filled me with a hope for all people, that all should come to know his forgiveness and be made righteous through the blood of Christ. This is the hope I must share, a race I must run. Since the moment I knelt in the dirt before Jesus, my hope has been that you, Shiri, would run this race with me.

I desire to see you rest in the knowledge of this truth: That Jesus, whom I persecuted, is raised from the dead; he is the Son of the living God, our Savior. Of this I have testified in my letters and witness to you now. In Barnabas and Silas, you have heard men of God proclaim the name of Jesus to you.

Therefore, Shiri, you have no excuse of ignorance before God. Yet, you remain steadfast in your opposition to the truth. And even though you have hardened your heart to what I preach, I would not renounce my vow to you on that account, as I would hope to win you over with time and patience. But if you will not remain with me, even in unbelief, I will not oppose your request. Let it be as you desire.

I do not say these things lightly. Though I am willing to endure great personal hardships to see Christ glorified, I did not foresee the loss of my wife being one of them. I am grateful to the compassion demonstrated by my new friends in Christ here in Damascus. They dried my tears with heartfelt prayers on our behalf and laying on of hands. They renewed my spirit and set my mind to the joy we have in Christ. And yet, no joy can come from divorce. It is not in keeping with God's commands or desires. But of this be certain: Though I release you from the bonds we share, I will not marry another. I remain bound in service to Christ Jesus. My devotion from this day forward will be to Christ and Christ alone.

Those who have sheltered me in Damascus make way for my departure this very evening. Therefore, I am dispatching this letter to you prior to leaving, as I lack confidence in their plan for my escape. While

I am uncertain of my fate, my confidence is in the Lord. Whether I am to remain in Damascus (free or in chains) or travel elsewhere, I trust he will use his servant for one purpose: to see Christ glorified.

Though I had planned to return to Jerusalem to see you and meet the other apostles of Christ, your letter persuades me otherwise. I will go where the Lord leads, but I need time to understand what has happened and how I may be of best use for Christ. A land distant from the controversy of my conversion may best suit this purpose for now. There I will learn to press on without you.

Greet your father, whom I hold in the highest regard, and other members of his household. Ask Ilan to return my tools to Haim. I will seek him out whenever I return to Jerusalem. And tell Jaron that I hold no ill will against him, for I am not the one to whom he will be made accountable for his actions.

My prayers for you will not cease, my dear Shiri, as long as I have breath within me. May you see the truth of my testimony and know the peace found in the one I serve.

Grace be with you, my love.

Paul

ABOUT THE AUTHOR

A native of South Carolina, Greg is a former IT professional and coffee shop owner. His four novels have received a total of twelve independent publishing book awards and honors. Having crafted relatable, realistic, and sometimes humorous character-driven stories in the Christian fiction genre with *A Seed for the Harvest* (2014) and *The Gills Creek Five* (2017), Greg explores coming-of-age themes in a 1974 summer beach setting in *The Sea Turtle* (2023). His latest work, *The Ballad of Walker Owens* (2024), is available in paperback, hardcover, Kindle, and Apple Books editions. While each of Greg's novels are unique in style and story, the savvy reader will note they share the same story universe. Greg earned both his bachelor's and master's degrees from the University of South Carolina and lives in Columbia, SC with his wife and two dogs.

www.ingramcontent.com/pod-product-compliance
Lightning Source LLC
Chambersburg PA
CBHW020611130626
46552CB00007B/3159